Soccer Stars

Written by
Jane Clarke

Illustrated by
Alan Brown

Earth's in the semi-finals
of the very first Worlds Cup!
It's Earth against the aliens.
Cup fever's building up.

Take a rocket to the Moon.
Put on Team Earth space suits.
Zoom into the stadium
in jetpack flying boots.

Team Mars will first play Saturn, then Earth will play Neptune. Robo Ref is ready for action on the Moon.

Watch the first semi-final!
Team Mars plays in a pattern.
They kick the ball in circles.
Then they run rings round Saturn.

Now, can Earth beat Neptune?
Both teams play defence.
The game goes into extra time.
Things are getting tense.

Neptune's team was icy cool,
but now they start to thaw.
They dribble over everyone.
Will it be a no-score draw?

Our goalie's looking nervous.
Go, Earth! What a save!
Earth has won the shoot-out!
Grab your flags and wave!

Earth is in the final!
Can we match the Martian's skill?
Get in there, Earth defenders.
Too late. Mars scores. One-nil.

Here's the equalizer!
Mars is seeing red.
Will they eat the referee?
Or tear him into shreds?

Robo's the best ref ever;
won't favour just one side.
A team can't cheat on Robo Ref;
no place in space to hide.

Four Martians are sent off the pitch!
The ref's still in control.
Go Earth! Just keep on scoring!
Goal … goal … goal … goal … goal … goooaaal!

Earth has won the Worlds Cup!
Set jetpack boots to 'zoom'.
Our players are the soccer stars.
We're all over the moon!